PIRATES vs. MONSTERS

Written by David Crosby

Illustrated by Lee Cosgrove

Three pirates met up at the old Parrot's Head,
To brag about **monsters** they'd each left for dead.

They boasted and laughed and drank lots of grog...

...While in from the sea crept a **blanket of fog.**

The first pirate, **Hector**, was tall, strong and **bold**,

And the teeth in his mouth were a **glimmering gold.**

"The **Hockler**," he bellowed, "could soar through the sky,
And spit globs of **poison** straight into your eye,
How did I beat it? You'll say the mind boggles!"

"With an arrow, a bow and a good pair of **goggles!**"

The pirates all **cackled**, tears rolled from their eyes,
While a ship nearing port, held a **frightful** surprise.

The next pirate, **Sue**, was a fearsome old girl,
With a **patch** on her eye, and her hair in a **curl**.

"The **Crunk**," she spat, "was a two-headed beast,
While one head would sleep, the other would **feast**."

"How did I beat it? With my **sneaking** skills!

I sprinkled its grub, with **crushed sleeping pills!**"

They all stamped their feet, with **horrible glee**...

...Outside from the ship, came
not one shape but **three**.

The last pirate, **George**, was round like an egg,
Under one of his knees, was a bright copper **peg**.

"The **Muncher**," he snarled,
"bites pirates on sight,
He **ate** my left leg but did not
get my right."

"How did I beat it? You're **desperate** to know!
I put pirate clothes on **a metal scarecrow!**"

They all laughed so hard that they fell to the floor...

...But their howls were drowned out by a **BANG** on the door!

The piano fell silent, replaced by a **SCREAM!**
Three **creatures** burst in, like a nightmarish dream!

Three **monsters** met up at the old Parrot's Head,
To brag about pirates they'd faced and had **fled**,
They boasted and laughed and got warm by the fire...

...But unlike the pirates, not one was a **LIAR!**